Adapted by
Tennant Redbank

Illustrated by
Jean-Paul Orpiñas
and
Scott Tilley

Designed by
Stuart Smith

DISNEY · PIXAR

A GOLDEN BOOK • NEW YORK

www.randomhouse.com/kids

Library of Congress Control Number: 2008934621

ISBN: 978-0-7364-2581-0

Printed in the United States of America

10 9 8 7 6 5

Carl Fredricksen lived alone in a little wooden house. He spent his days with his memories of his wife, Ellie.

But all around him, things were changing. People wanted Carl to leave his house so they could put up more buildings. So Carl came up with a plan.

Hundreds of balloons lifted Carl's house into the air. He had tied the balloons to the house so that he could fly away.

UP!

UP!

UP!

Carl steered the house south. He was heading for Paradise Falls in South America. His wife, Ellie, had always wanted to go there.

Suddenly, Carl heard a sound. *Knock! Knock! Knock!* Carl opened the door. A boy named Russell was on the front porch. Like it or not, Carl had company for his trip!

Russell was a Junior Wilderness Explorer. He had earned badges for fishing, camping, and many other things.

In fact, he had earned every badge
there was—except for the
Assisting the Elderly badge.

So Russell held on tight.
The house flew through a storm.

It flew through fog.

Then . . . *CRASH!*
The house bumped
on the ground. Carl
and Russell rolled off
the porch.

Carl barely managed to catch the house before it floated away.

In the distance, Carl could see Paradise Falls. He and Russell would have to walk to the falls, pulling the house behind them with a long garden hose.

On the way to the falls, Russell found weird tracks in the mud. They belonged to a bird—a strange, HUGE, colorful bird! Russell named the bird Kevin.

It was bad enough that
Carl had to put up with a
Junior Wilderness
Explorer. He didn't need
a HUGE bird, too.
"Scram!" Carl said.
Kevin followed them anyway.

Kevin wasn't the only odd creature they met. Next, Carl and Russell found a dog.

"Hi there," said the dog. "My name is Dug." Carl and Russell were shocked. The dog could talk!

Dug was on a mission to bring the bird to his master. But Carl promised Russell that he would protect Kevin.

And as it turned out, Kevin was a mother! She had baby birds waiting for her at home.

Nothing was going the way Carl had planned. He now had a floating house, a talking dog, a Junior Wilderness Explorer, and a HUGE bird. Whatever happened to being alone with just his house and his memories of Ellie?

The next morning, three fierce dogs
burst from the bushes.

They surrounded Carl, Russell, and
Dug. Like Dug, the dogs had been sent
on a mission to find the bird.

Luckily, Kevin was hiding.

The dogs took Carl and Russell to their master, Charles Muntz.

Carl found out that Muntz had spent years trying to capture the bird.

Carl remembered his promise to Russell. He had to protect Kevin and get her back to her babies. Dug helped them escape.

But Muntz caught them. He took
Carl's house and set it on fire!

In the end, Carl let Muntz
take Kevin so he could save
his house. He loved it too
much to let it burn.

Carl made it to Paradise Falls.
But he felt lonely in his empty house.
So, with Russell and Dug's
help, Carl went back and
rescued Kevin.

But this time, Carl could not save his house.

It fell DOWN.

Down.

Down.

But that was okay. Carl might have lost his house, but he still had his memories of Ellie. And he also had friends.